The Hospital Caper

The Adventures of Callie Ann

Summer Surprise
The Ballet Class Mystery
The Hospital Caper
The Miss Kitty Mystery

The Hospital Caper

Shannon Mason Leppard

BETHANY HOUSE PUBLISHERS
MINNEAPOLIS, MINNESOTA 55438

Published by Bethany House Publishers
A Ministry of Bethany Fellowship, Inc.
11300 Hampshire Avenue South
Minneapolis, Minnesota 55438

Printed in the United States of America.

Library of Congress Cataloging-in-Publication Data

Leppard, Shannon Mason.
    The hospital caper / by Shannon Mason Leppard.
       p. cm. — (The adventures of Callie Ann ; 3)
    Summary: When Callie and her mother make a trip back to Greenville, North Carolina, to see Grandmama, who is in the hospital, Callie learns that God hears her no matter where she is.
    ISBN 1–55661–815–8 (pbk.)
    [1. Grandmothers—Fiction. 2. Hospitals—Fiction.
3. Christian life—Fiction. 4. Friendship—Fiction.] I. Title.
II. Series: Leppard, Shannon Mason. Adventures of Callie Ann ; 3.
PZ7.L5565Ho   1997
[Fic]—dc21   97–21040
                                       CIP
                                       AC

For my own sweet grandmother,
Florence George Tucker,
I love you always.
Also for our family doctor,
Dr. James Peckinpaush,
Thank you!

SHANNON MASON LEPPARD grew up in a small town in South Carolina, where summer days were spent under the shade of an old weeping willow tree and winters under the quilting frames of her grandmother. Shannon brings her flair for drama and make-believe to THE ADVENTURES OF CALLIE ANN, her first series with Bethany House. She and her husband, Donn, make their home in North Carolina along with their two teenage daughters.

Chapter One

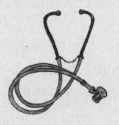

Sunday morning was getting off to a hot start when Callie Ann Davies woke up.

"Good morning, Miss Kitty! Are you ready to go outside?" Callie asked her big black cat. It seemed to Callie that Miss Kitty was getting a lot bigger everyday, but her mom said it was just because Miss Kitty didn't do anything.

Miss Kitty jumped down from Callie's nice soft bed and stretched. Callie started out of the room and called back, "Come on, Miss Kitty. I know it's hot, but you really do need to go out now. Come on!"

With that, Miss Kitty ran past Callie down the steps and into the kitchen. Callie was about to let the cat out the back door when her mom came into the kitchen.

"Morning, Mom! I need to let Miss Kitty out. We'll be right back in," Callie said as she opened the back door.

"Don't be long. Your pancakes will be ready in just a short while," Mom answered.

Callie and Miss Kitty went out the back door and into the heat. "Boy, Miss Kitty, it sure is hot out here," Callie said as Miss Kitty ran across the backyard.

"Morning, Callie," Jason called from his yard. "It sure is hot, ain't it?" He was out with his all-white cat, Jack. Callie still thought Jack was a strange name for a cat, but then again, he was Jason's cat. And Jason was a *boy*.

"Sure is. Miss Kitty didn't want to come out because it's so hot." Callie made her way across the yard.

"I hope the air conditioning is on at the church," Jason said. "It was so hot last week in Sunday school. I thought we'd all burn up."

"It's on. Daddy went over to turn it down some more. He should be back by now. Well, Miss Kitty, let's go in and eat. See you at church,

Jason. 'Bye, Jack." Callie picked up Miss Kitty and started toward the house.

"Miss Kitty, we are going to have to put you on a diet," Callie said, lifting the heavy cat to her shoulder. They made their way across the backyard just as Callie's daddy pulled up in the driveway.

"Good morning, ladies. How are my girls this morning?" Daddy asked as he scratched behind Miss Kitty's ears.

"We're fine, Daddy. Mom's making pancakes this morning." Callie smiled up at him.

"That's wonderful," Daddy said as he opened the back door of their old farmhouse.

❦❦❦

"You'd better hurry and get dressed, Callie," Mom instructed when Callie was finished with breakfast and had put her plate in the sink. "Make sure you brush your teeth. And *please* pull your hair back in a ponytail."

"I might need help doing my hair," Callie said. Callie had lots of red hair that never did what is was supposed to do.

"Oh, good! I love doing your hair," Daddy

called after Callie as she left the kitchen. "I'll just run out to the barn and get the garden rake."

"Funny, Daddy. Very funny," Callie called back.

Just as Callie started up the steps, Miss Kitty ran past her. "Boy, you sure do move fast when you want to take a nap in the tub." Miss Kitty's favorite place to sleep was the bathtub.

"When I come back from church, Miss Kitty, you and I are going for a walk. I think you've gotten way too big for a cat. You're more in the small dog size now."

Miss Kitty gave Callie a very mean look and then curled up in the bathtub to go to sleep.

Callie was trying to pull her hair into a ponytail when the phone rang. She knew her mom or daddy would get it. It was always somebody from church needing a ride or something like that.

Callie could hear her mom on the phone in the hall outside of Callie's bedroom. She thought she heard her say something to Callie's uncle Danny. *Why is Uncle Danny calling on a Sunday morning?* Callie wondered. She stepped out of her room to find out.

Callie stood there listening for a few minutes. It had to be Uncle Danny. Mom had said something about the hospital in Greenville. What was going on?

"Callie, honey, would you please go get Daddy for me?" Mom asked. She had a very worried look on her face. "I think he's in the study."

Callie hurried down the steps. Was someone sick? Uncle Danny wouldn't be calling unless something was really wrong.

Callie found her daddy right where Mom said he would be. "Oh, Daddy, Mom wants you right away. Something's wrong. Uncle Danny is on the phone. And I heard her say something about the hospital." Callie said it all in one breath.

They ran back up the steps to where Mom was still on the phone.

"Mom, what's wrong?" Callie asked as she sat down in the green armchair that was next to the hall phone.

"Wait until she's off the phone. Then she can tell us," Daddy said.

It seemed to Callie that her mom was on the

phone *forever*. She said something about getting there as soon as she could. And something about Grandmama. . . .

What could have happened to Grandmama?

Chapter Two

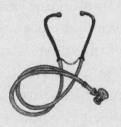

Finally, Mom hung up the phone. "It seems that Grandmama fell this morning, Callie," she explained. "They don't know right now how bad she's hurt or if anything's broken. So Uncle Danny wants me to come down. I told him I'd be there as soon as I could."

"You go right ahead," Daddy said. "David and I will come down there tomorrow morning." He gave Mom a hug. "If you need me, I can come down right after morning service."

"I'll let you know. Callie, I need for you to pack a few things. You can stay with Meghan Johnson overnight if need be," Mom said.

"Why do I have to stay with Meg?" Callie wailed at the top of her voice. "Grandmama needs me if she's hurt. I can't go over to Meg's house." Callie liked Meghan—after all, she was her best friend in the whole world, or at least in Greenville. But Grandmama might need Callie.

"Callie Ann, you'll do as your mother asked," Daddy said in a firm voice. "And don't give her any trouble, or you'll have to stay here with David and me until tomorrow."

"Yes, sir," Callie answered. *I might not like it,* she thought to herself, *but at least I'll do it.*

Callie went back into her room to put a few things in a bag to take to Greenville. Miss Kitty had gotten out of the tub and was now on Callie's bed with her head propped on a stuffed bear. "Miss Kitty, Grandmama is sick," Callie explained. "Mom and I are going down to see her. I have to make Grandmama better. She always made me feel better when I was sick."

Callie went to the closet to get her spend-the-night bag that Grandmama had given her right before they moved from Greenville to Cornelius. When she went to open the bag, a note fell out.

"Look, Miss Kitty, a note," Callie said, pulling the green paper out of the bag. "Grandmama must have put it in the bag for me to find." Callie unfolded the piece of paper. Sure enough, it was a note from Grandmama.

"Listen, Miss Kitty. 'To my sweet Callie Ann. Always remember I love you and that no matter how far you go I'll always be with thinking of you. Remember our saying: Look to your heart and you'll never go wrong. You be a sweet girl. Love you bunches. . . . Grandmama.' "

Callie didn't say anything for a few minutes. She just sat and looked at the note as tears ran down her face. *That's it*, she thought to herself. *I've got to go to the hospital. I can't stay with Meg. If Grandmama needs me, I'll be there.*

Callie hurried and packed what she thought she'd need in Greenville. Miss Kitty wasn't sure what was going on. She just stayed on the bed under the fan.

"You be a good cat. I'll get Daddy to let you out after he comes back from church," Callie told Miss Kitty. "I'll be home soon."

Callie picked up her bag and ran down to the kitchen, where her mom was putting away the breakfast dishes.

"Honey, your daddy wants to tell you something," she said. "He's in his study."

Callie ran into her daddy's study. He was sitting at his big desk with his hands folded in prayer. She sat down beside him to say a prayer, too.

"Dear God, please hear my prayer. My Grandmama is hurt, and she needs your help. I'm not asking for me. I'm asking for Papa. I'm not sure what he'd do if Grandmama was real bad. So please look after her. Let her know that I'm coming. And let her know how much I love her. Amen. Oh, and thank you for all our blessings. . . . Amen again."

"That was very nice, Callie. I'm sure God will look after Grandmama. Now, you need to be very good for your mom. She has a lot on her mind. And she doesn't need you to pull any tricks while you're down in Greenville." Daddy held Callie's hand in his.

"I'll be real good, Daddy. I promise. Mom will be real proud of me, 'cause I'll help Grandmama so much." Callie smiled from ear to ear.

"All right, Callie. I'm counting on you to do just that. I love you." Daddy gave her a big hug.

"I love you, too, Daddy. Mom and I really

have to go. Grandmama needs us," Callie said as they left the study.

"Mom, I'm ready! Are you?"

"I guess. I think we have everything taken care of," Mom answered. "Oh, I forgot about David."

"Daddy will take care of him, Mom. He's a big boy." Callie picked up her spend-the-night bag and started out to the car.

"I sure will take care of David. You two be *very* careful. I'll call as soon as we get out of church. 'Bye now. Love you both," Daddy called as Callie and her mom put their things into the Jeep for the two-hour trip to Greenville.

"'Bye. We love you, too," Mom called back as she helped Callie put her seat belt on. "Well, Callie, we're off."

As they backed out of the driveway, Callie could see Daddy waving from the back porch. Then she saw Jason coming across the backyard. She should have called Jason and told him she was leaving. Oh well, Daddy would tell him everything.

Callie usually didn't mind going to Greenville. The trip wasn't very long. And she always knew she would see a lot of people when she got there.

But this time was different. Two hours was a long time to wait to see Grandmama. And she really didn't want to see anyone else.

"Mom, can we stop at that little store that we always stop at? I could get Grandmama some candy. And if they have 'em, I could get her some flowers."

"Not this time, honey," Mom said. "We'll stop only if you need to go to the bathroom or need a drink. Otherwise, I think we just need to hurry on down to Grandmama."

"OK, Mom. I guess I can wait till we get down there to get her some flowers," Callie answered.

Callie tried to be still, but it was hard knowing Grandmama was sick. Jason had told Callie that his family was going to drive to Missouri later in the summer to see his grandma. Callie didn't see how anybody could ride that long. Thank goodness her grandmama lived only two hours away. But now two hours seemed to take all day.

Chapter Three

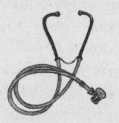

Callie must have fallen asleep because the next thing she saw was the exit for Greenville coming up on the highway.

"Well, hello! Did you have a nice nap?" Mom asked.

"I guess," Callie said, rubbing the sleep out of her eyes. "I'm sorry, Mom. I was going to keep you company. But I fell asleep."

"That's OK, Callie. You got a nap and will be ready to play with Meghan this afternoon while I'm at the hospital," Mom replied.

"I can't play with Meg! I've got to go to Grandmama!" Callie cried in a big voice that was even louder than she meant it to be.

"Callie Ann Davies, *do not* yell in this car," Mom scolded.

"I'm sorry, Mom," Callie said in her best I'm-sorry voice. "I didn't mean to yell. It just came out before my brain could stop it. But I really have to see Grandmama."

"Honey, I don't think the hospital will let you in," Mom said. "You have to be twelve to go see anybody in the hospital. Would you rather stay at Aunt Debbie's instead of going to Meg's?"

"I guess I'll go play at Meg's," Callie said in a very low voice. "That way you, Uncle Danny, and Aunt Debbie can stay with Grandmama."

The next several minutes Callie tried to think of a way to get into the hospital. *I know*, she thought to herself. *I'll get Mom to see if Meg's mom can pick me up from the hospital. That way maybe I can sneak in before anybody sees me.*

"Mom, could you call and see if Mrs. Johnson can pick me up from the hospital? That way maybe I can see Uncle Danny and Aunt Debbie before I go over to Meg's." Callie smiled to herself.

"I guess I can do that," Mom replied. "I'll try to get her on the car phone."

While Mom was calling Mrs. Johnson, Callie thought to herself, *I know there must be a way to get in to see Grandmama. I wish Jason was here. He'd find a way in. He's real good at things like this.*

"OK, Miss Callie Ann. Here's the hospital. Mrs. Johnson said she'll get here as soon as she can," Mom said.

Great, Callie thought. *Now I'll have time to get to Grandmama's room to see her.*

They went into the front door of the hospital and up to the information desk. Callie recognized the lady behind the desk. Mrs. Tate was from their old church.

"Hello, Mrs. Davies and Miss Callie. I knew you two would be here sometime today." Mrs. Tate smiled at Callie.

"Well, hello!" Callie's mom said. "Yes, Callie and I had to come. My mom is here. Callie is going home with Meghan Johnson for the afternoon."

"Your brother just called down to see if you were here. He said your mother was going to X-ray. Miss Callie will be fine right here with me until Meghan and Mrs. Johnson get here." Mrs.

Tate gave Callie a hug. "Callie and Meg were in my Sunday school class when they were four. I think I can handle her for a while. So you go ahead."

"It's OK, Mom. You go see Grandmama." Callie was smiling. This was working out better than she thought it would. Mom would go to Grandmama's room first. Then Callie could sneak in.

"Well, if you're sure you don't mind, Mrs. Tate. I really would like to see my mother now." Callie's mom put her hand on Callie's back. "Now, Callie, please don't give Mrs. Tate any trouble. Meg and Mrs. Johnson should be here soon. I'll call you when I get ready to go to Grandmama's house this afternoon."

"All right, Mom. I'll be good." Callie gave her mom a half smile.

Callie watched her mom go into the hallway that led to Grandmama's room. Then she turned and asked Mrs. Tate what her grandmama's room number was.

"Well, let's see, honey—here it is. Room 104. Oh now, don't you worry your pretty little head. Your grandmama will be just fine." Mrs. Tate gave Callie another hug.

The phones were ringing a lot. And Mrs. Tate was busy telling visitors where to find the patients they wanted to see. Callie stayed right beside Mrs. Tate. Her desk was next to the door that led to the first floor. And that was where Grandmama was.

Somehow, Callie thought, *I have to get in that door and down to the other end of the hall. I think Grandmama is in the room right across the hall from the room I was in when I fell off my bike and hurt my arm.*

"Callie, honey, you wait right here. I'll be right back. I need to put this file in the office across the hall. Won't take me a minute." Mrs. Tate smiled down at Callie.

"OK, Mrs. Tate," Callie said. *Now's the time*, she thought. *Just through the door and down the hall. Then I can wait for Grandmama to get back to her room.*

As soon as Mrs. Tate was out of sight, Callie pulled the big double doors open. *So far so good*, Callie thought. *No one in the hall. Now I'll just make my way down a little farther.*

Callie could see the big desk where the nurses stay, but she didn't see anybody there. But then she saw a shadow. "Oh no, somebody's coming!" Callie said out loud.

Chapter Four

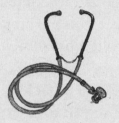

She ducked into a small space beside the water fountain. She had to stay there for what must have been a good three minutes.

Whew! That was close. I need to move a little faster, Callie thought. She was moving closer to the nurses' desk when she heard a voice coming from behind her.

"Hi, where are you going?" the voice said.

Callie turned around real slow. It was a little girl in a wheelchair.

"Well, I'm trying to get down the hall to see my grandmama without anyone seeing me," Callie explained.

"Oh, I see. You're not supposed to be in here."

"My Grandmama needs me. I have to be in here," Callie said.

A man came out of one of the rooms and called for the little girl to come back inside.

"I hope you get to see your grandmama," the girl said as she rolled herself back to her room. " 'Bye now."

" 'Bye," Callie called back to her. "And thank you. I will get to see Grandmama."

Callie started to make her way back down the hall. When she had started, the hall didn't look so long. Now it looked like it might be a mile or two. Callie made her way past a lot of open doorways and past the nurses' desk before she had to hide again. This time a huge potted fern was her hiding place.

I can't believe I'm standing behind a plant that's taller than I am, Callie fussed to herself. *But it's worth it. 'Cause I need to get to Grandmama.*

Just as Callie came out from behind the plant, the little girl came rolling up again.

"Hi again. My name is Jamie," the girl said.

"Hi, Jamie. I'm Callie." Callie thought the girl was about six or seven years old.

"Wanna know why I'm here?" Jamie asked.

"Sure, I guess. If you want to tell me." Callie wanted to get rid of the girl so she could go see Grandmama.

"Well, I got real sick about two years ago. Now I'm getting my tonsils out," Jamie said.

"Your tonsils out!" Callie exclaimed. "They can do that? I mean, don't you need those?"

"Oh no, you can do fine without them." Jamie didn't seem worried at all.

"You mean they are just going to take them out?" Callie didn't understand how that could be.

"Sure. And the best part is I get to eat all the ice cream I want. And they let me play with this wheelchair." The man Callie had seen before came down the hall to get Jamie again. "Gotta go, Callie. It's time for me to rest now. 'Bye again."

With that, Jamie was gone down the hall and into her room. *Wow*, Callie thought. *All the ice cream she wants.*

Callie started down the hall again. She was getting closer to another nurses' desk. This time at least four or five people were at the desk.

Now, how am I going to get past them? Callie wondered.

There was a small space in front of a door marked *Supply Closet.* Callie stood very still in the doorway, thinking about what to do.

She stood there until there was only one person left at the desk. And she was sitting down typing. *Great,* Callie thought. *Now, if I can do a really good duck walk and go right past the desk without her seeing me, I'll be home free.*

Callie stooped down and started to walk like a duck. "Just a little farther," she said out loud. "Boy, this is hard. I don't see how ducks can do this all the time."

"Me either," a voice said from behind her.

"Jamie, is that you?" Callie asked softly without turning around.

"No, not Jamie," the voice said.

"Well, are you a big person?" Callie asked.

"Not too big, I guess. Even though some people say I am," the voice said.

"OK. Am . . . am I in trouble?" Callie still didn't turn around. She wasn't sure if she wanted to know.

"I don't know. *Are* you?" the voice said.

"I think I need to see who you are now. OK, here I go. I'm turning around." Callie slowly stood up and turned around to see who the voice belonged to.

Chapter Five

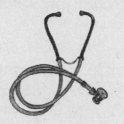

"DR. JAMES! It's just you!" Callie exclaimed.

"Well, hello, Miss Callie." The tall man laughed.

"I'm happy to see you. Have you been behind me long?" Callie asked, hugging the doctor.

"Well, if you count both times you've talked to Jamie and the time behind the potted plant, I'd say yes." Doctor James smiled.

"I didn't think anybody saw me." Callie looked down at her shoes.

"So tell me, little miss, what are you doing in the hospital?" the doctor asked.

Callie told him all about how Grandmama was hurt and how Uncle Danny had called for her mom to come down. "But, Dr. James, they won't let me in to see her. Something about having to be twelve. Have you ever heard of such a thing?" Callie put both hands on her hips.

"All hospitals have rules, Callie," Dr. James said. "I know they're not any fun. Mrs. Tate told me you were sneaking down the hall, so I thought I'd see just how far you could get on your own."

"Please let me make it all the way to Room 104," Callie pleaded. "I want to make sure Grandmama is all right. Then I'll go back to Mrs. Tate and wait for Meg to come pick me up."

"Hold on, missy. I'll call back to the desk to see if your friend is here yet. Then I'll walk you down to see your grandmama if you promise we don't have to duck walk. I'm way to old for that." Dr. James held his back like it hurt.

"OH, THANK YOU! THANK YOU!" Callie yelled.

"Pipe down, little person! Boy, you sure can yell for someone so small," Dr. James said, shaking his head and smiling.

While the doctor called Mrs. Tate, Callie saw another doctor go into Jamie's room. *I hope she's going to be all right*, Callie thought.

Dr. James hung up the phone and turned to Callie. "Well, Callie, Meg and her mom aren't here yet. Mrs. Tate told me your grandmama is just finishing up in X-ray. So you and I can talk a few minutes before she gets back to her room. Now, what were you doing, the duck walk?" he asked.

"Yes, sir. Do you remember when we had Amy's birthday party at the pool at y'all's house? You said we all had to duck walk or we couldn't have any cake," Callie said.

Amy was Dr. James' daughter. She was a year older than Callie. Amy, Callie, and Meghan had been best friends for as long as Callie could remember. *Now I don't get to see them very much*, Callie thought.

"Oh yes, I had forgotten all about the ducks walking around at Amy's party. But we did have a good time," Dr. James said.

"Yeah, I miss Amy and Meg. But I have a new friend in Cornelius. His name is Jason Alexander," Callie replied.

"A *boy*! Oh no, what is the world coming to?" Dr. James laughed. "Well, I'm sure he's a good friend."

"He is. And he likes to ride his bike as much as I like to ride mine," Callie answered. Just then Callie saw a doctor come out of Jamie's room and make a phone call.

"Dr. James, do you know Jamie?" Callie asked.

"Sure do. She's a real sweet little girl," he said.

"She told me that she was getting her tonsils out. Can you really do that?" Callie asked.

"Sure can. Doctors can do a lot of wonderful things now. Dr. Mac is waiting for the information to get here from Atlanta. That's where Jamie and her family moved from. Dr. Mac needs her medical records," Dr. James explained.

"Atlanta. Boy, I bet she misses her friends a lot," Callie thought out loud.

"I'm sure she does. But I know she'll make lots of new friends here in Greenville," Dr. James said.

"Dr. James," Callie said. "Is Grandmama

going to be all right?" She could feel the tears in her eyes.

"Oh, my goodness, yes, Callie. Your grandmama just broke her ankle. She'll be up and around before you know it. Are you ready to go see for yourself?" He gave Callie a hug.

Callie and Dr. James started down the hall just as Dr. Mac wheeled Jamie into the hall.

"Jamie," Callie called. "I know you're going to get better. Dr. James told me so. He says he knows Dr. Mac, so you'll be great."

"Thanks, Callie. I hope your grandmama is all right. Maybe you can see me after I get out," Jamie said as the doctor rolled her wheelchair into a small room.

Callie couldn't help worrying about Jamie. She was so little.

"Doctor James, do you think it would be OK to say a prayer for Jamie?" Callie asked.

"Why, Callie, I think that would be a great idea. We have a chapel just off to the side up here. You and I will stop and both say a prayer for Jamie. We'll also say a prayer for Dr. Mac and your grandmama. How's that?" Dr. James took Callie's hand and brought her into the chapel. It was small and quiet and had a little window that looked out into the garden.

"Callie, do you want to start or should I?" Doctor James asked.

"I will, please," Callie answered.

"That's fine with me, Callie." He folded his hands.

Callie closed her eyes and bowed her head. "Dear God, it's me, Callie Ann Davies. I know I talk to you a lot. But I want to make sure you don't miss anything. Anyway, Dr. James is with me so you won't have to worry about me getting lost in this hospital. He said Grandmama is going to be fine. I'll get to see her in a few minutes. Do you know Jamie? I guess you know everybody. Well, I just met her. The doctor told me what was wrong with her. Could you please look out for her and help her get well? Look after Dr. Mac, too. He's the one who is going to help Jamie. I've gotta go now. I'm going to see Grandmama. Thank you for *all* our blessings. And watch over Jamie and her mom and dad. Amen."

When Dr. James finished saying his prayer, Callie looked up to see the sun coming through

the stained-glass window. The light was so bright that it looked like the angel on the window was flying.

"Look, Dr. James. It looks like the angel is flying back to tell God about Jamie," Callie exclaimed.

Dr. James looked up at the window. "Well, Callie, you asked that He watch over Jamie. So maybe He sent that angel to do just that. We'd better go. Your grandmama is waiting for you."

They got up and went back into the hall. But Callie had to look back just once more to see if the angel was still there.

"Dr. James," Callie started. "Do you believe that God can hear us no matter where we are?"

"Oh, Callie, I do hope He can. Because there are a lot of times I have to 'pray on the run,' as I call it," Dr. James said.

"Well, you're in luck. My brother said He could, and David does not lie."

Callie glanced into most of the rooms as they went down the hall. There sure were a lot of sick people. Most of them were older people. Somehow Callie couldn't stop thinking of how Jamie was so little yet so brave. *I'll just have to stop by to see her before we go back home*, Callie thought.

Chapter Six

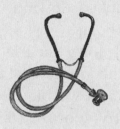

"Well, here we are, Miss Callie. Are you ready?" Dr. James asked when they reached Room 104.

"Boy, am I ever," Callie said, pushing open the big door that went into Grandmama's room.

"Callie Ann Davies—" Mom started.

"But, Mom," Callie said. "I really had to see Grandmama. Dr. James was with me most of the time, and I met a little girl named Jamie and she's real sick and—"

Callie's mom put her hands up in the shape of a T, meaning time out. Callie was silent.

"I know you wanted to see Grandmama. I was going to come back and get you as soon as we were out of X-ray. The nurses were going to make an exception for you. You really didn't have to get Dr. James in on all this. You should have just waited," Callie's mom scolded.

Callie just looked down at her shoes until Grandmama spoke up.

"Well, Sara, I don't think Dr. James minded helping Callie. She just needed to see that I was all right. Sometimes we big people forget that little people worry, too. Isn't that right, Callie?" Grandmama held her arms out to Callie.

"Mom, I'm sorry. I know I wasn't supposed to leave the front hall where Mrs. Tate was. But I really did need to see Grandmama," Callie said as she hugged Grandmama tight.

"We'll have to talk about this later, Callie Ann. Right now Meg and her mom are probably waiting for you out front." Mom still sounded upset. Callie didn't want to look at her. She knew what she had done was wrong. But Grandmama did have a point. Sometimes big people did forget how little people felt.

"OK, Mom. Grandmama, I'm so happy that you are going to be all right," Callie said, hugging Grandmama again. "I was so worried about you. I remembered you had been with me when

I was sick. So I had to come to you."

"Now that you know I'm fine, you can go play with Meghan. The doctor said he'll let me go home in the morning. You can spend the night at my house. How's that?" Grandmama let go of Callie and looked in her eyes.

"OK, little miss, it's time you and I walk back down to the front desk to find Meg," Mom said.

"Don't worry, Callie. I'll take good care of your grandmama. You have a good time now," Dr. James said as Callie and her mom went out the door of Grandmama's room.

"I know you will, Dr. James. Can you watch out for Jamie, too?" Callie stopped to ask.

"Sure will. I'll let your mom know how she is before she leaves the hospital today. Is that OK for ya?" Dr. James squeezed Callie's shoulder.

"That would be super. Tell Amy I said hello. 'Bye, Grandmama, I love you," Callie called back into the room.

Now I better make sure Mom isn't too mad at me, Callie thought. "Mom," she said, "I really am sorry. I didn't mean to upset you or make you mad. I just wanted to see Grandmama. And I made a friend along the way. Her name is

Jamie." Callie hoped that if she talked enough, Mom wouldn't be too mad at her for not minding.

"Callie, you know I asked you to stay with Mrs. Tate. You didn't do that. So, yes, I am upset with you. I also understand that you needed to see your Grandmama. I just wish you would have waited for me to come get you," Mom told Callie.

"Yes, ma'am," Callie said.

"You're going over to Meghan's now until six or so. Then I'll come and get you. We can bring supper up to Grandmama. How does that sound?"

"That would be fantastic. I wonder if Mrs. Johnson would let me make brownies at her house for Grandmama." Callie looked up at her mom.

"I'm sure we could ask. Now tell me about Jamie," Mom said as she and Callie walked down the long hall to where Mrs. Tate was.

"She's real small, Mom. She has to have her tonsils out. I don't know what's wrong with them. Dr. James said she could do without hers, though. He said she'll be all right."

"Well, Callie, I'm glad you got to meet Jamie," Mom said. "I'm sure if Dr. James said she'll be all right, then she will. You know that Dr. James is a very good doctor."

"I know, Mom. Do you think when I come back to have supper with Grandmama I could stop in to see Jamie?" Callie asked.

"We'll see."

They walked the rest of the way down the hall without talking. Callie kept thinking about Jamie. She thought Jamie was awfully small to have to be in the hospital.

Chapter Seven

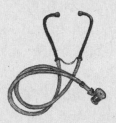

Mrs. Johnson and Meghan were waiting for Callie at the front desk.

"Well, there you are!" Mrs. Tate said. "Dr. James said he'd walk with you. I guess he caught up with you all right?"

"Yes, ma'am. He did. I'm sorry I didn't stay where you told me to," Callie apologized. "I just really needed to see Grandmama."

"No harm done, Callie. How is your grandmama?"

"She's wonderful. She broke her ankle, but Dr. James said she can go home in the morning." Callie beamed.

"OK, Miss Callie Ann," Mom said. "You go with Mrs. Johnson and Meg now. I'll call you around four, and we'll plan what to have for supper. Please be a sweet girl."

Callie could tell what her mom was thinking—*Don't get into anything*.

"I'll be better than good, Mom. I promise," Callie said. "You take care of Grandmama. I'll see you in a while. I love you!"

"Love you, too, Callie." Mom turned to Meg's mom. "Thank you, Mrs. Johnson, for coming to pick her up. I don't know what we would have done without you."

Callie couldn't wait to tell Meg all about Jamie. She also needed to ask about making brownies at their house. Oh well, they'd have all afternoon to talk and to play. Right now Callie was hungry.

"Mrs. Johnson, could we stop and get something to eat?" Callie asked. "I haven't eaten in a while, and I'm hungry."

"I think that sounds like a good idea. You two decide where," Mrs. Johnson said.

"Oh, Callie, what about that place down by Cunningham Lake? The Swamp Rat," Meg said in a loud voice.

Callie squealed in delight. "Yes! Yes! I love

The Swamp Rat. We can have the Swamp Thing."

"Wait a minute, you two. Just what is a Swamp Thing?" Mrs. Johnson asked.

Both girls laughed, and Callie said, "It's just a big hamburger with chili on it, with curly fries and a large Swamp Drink—better known as a cherry Coke."

"Well, three Swamp Things it is." Mrs. Johnson laughed, too.

All the way to The Swamp Rat Callie told Meghan and Mrs. Johnson about Jamie and how Grandmama was doing. Meg even asked about Jason. Callie knew now that Meg really did like Jason. But that was OK with her. Callie had learned that you could never have too many friends.

Callie, Meghan, and Mrs. Johnson ate their Swamp Things and laughed at the ducks.

"I really like coming here," Callie said. "You can eat and see the lake at the same time. Look at all the sailboats!"

There must have been six or seven sailboats on the lake. All with pretty, brightly colored sails. Callie had been sailing only once before. But she knew she'd like to do it again someday.

Grandmama had taken her and David to Lake Cunningham about two summers ago to go sailing with a group from church. Callie had loved it. *I'll wait until Grandmama is better, then I'll get her to go with me again,* Callie thought as she ate her burger.

"Would you two like to go on the paddle boats?" Mrs. Johnson asked.

"Oh boy, I'd love to," Callie exclaimed. "How about you, Meg?"

"Sure, let me finish eating. Thank you, Mom!" Meghan added.

As soon as Meghan was finished and Mrs. Johnson paid the bill, they all walked around the side of The Swamp Rat to where the paddle boats were kept. Callie had done this before with her parents. It looked like they had gotten a few more boats since Callie had been there.

"Come on, you two. Let's get a boat and go out," Mrs. Johnson said, taking their hands.

"Which boat do you want, Callie? I like the yellow one with the ladybugs on it," Meghan said.

"That one looks good to me. Are you ready, Mrs. Johnson?" Callie asked.

"Sure. Are you two going to do all the paddling?" Mrs. Johnson asked as she paid the man for the use of the boat.

"Great, I'd love to. Maybe this time I won't make it go around in a circle like I did with my mom," Callie said.

Callie, Meg, and Mrs. Johnson got on the yellow paddle boat and started out of the holding area to the open water of Lake Cunningham.

"Boy, this is great. Don't you love this, Meg?" Callie asked.

"Yeah, this is really fun. Oh, watch out, Callie. We're going to run into the sandbar," Meghan said as she pedaled faster to turn the small boat.

Callie and Meghan laughed so hard that their sides hurt. Time went by way too fast for Callie. Soon it was time to take their boat in and go to Meghan's house.

"Thank you, Mrs. Johnson. That was fun," Callie said as they walked back to the car. "Oh, Mrs. Johnson, do you think Meg and I could make brownies at your house? My grandmama loves 'em. I thought if you'd let us we could make some for her."

"I think that would be wonderful," Mrs. Johnson said. "I'll help you, and then you and Meg can play awhile before your mom comes to get you. How's that?"

"Thank you again. You're almost like my mom," Callie said, smiling up at the pretty lady. Then she turned to her friend. "Meg, I have to tell you all about ballet and the new boy I met. His name is Sean, and he can't hear."

Callie told Meghan all about the dance their class did at the nursing home and how wonderfully Sean could dance, even without hearing.

Chapter Eight

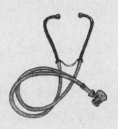

"We're here, Callie," Meghan said when they pulled into the Johnsons' driveway. "You have to see my bedroom. Mom let me paint it pale lavender with white clouds on the ceiling. You'll love it," Meghan said.

"Oh, I can't wait. Mom said we could repaint mine sometime soon. Maybe I can do it like yours. That way we'll feel like we're together," Callie said, taking off her seat belt.

Callie and Meghan ran ahead of Mrs. Johnson to the front door of the small white house. Callie liked Meg's house. It had a dark green front door, and the porch rockers were painted to match.

Mrs. Johnson unlocked the door—with a

little help from Mr. Kitty, who was on the inside playing with the doorknob.

"Look, Meg. Mr. Kitty is trying to let us in," Callie said, looking through the window on the door.

"He's funny. He even tried to help Mom and me paint. You should have seen his paws. We still have a few paw prints on the floor outside my room." Meg laughed.

Once inside, they went to see Meghan's new room. It sure was pretty, with a white bedspread and white curtains. *I hope Mom will let me do this to my room*, Callie thought.

"Girls, I have everything ready for making brownies. Do you want to do it now or wait awhile?" Mrs. Johnson called from down the hall.

"What do you think, Callie. Now or later?" Meghan asked.

"Now's good. I want to do the brownies before Mom calls and I have to go back to the hospital." Callie began spinning around and around in the room. "I love your room. I hope Mom lets me paint mine."

"Let's go," Meghan said. "We'll make the

brownies and then go for a ride. You can ride my bike. I'll ride Mom's."

Callie stayed behind for a minute just to look at how different Meghan's room looked. She really liked the colors. It was the same color as the room she had at Grandmama's house.

"Callie, you ready?" Meghan stuck her head back in the bedroom door.

"Yep, I'm ready. It's nice of your mom to let me make the brownies for Grandmama. You know, I really do miss Grandmama a lot. But now I miss home and Jason," Callie said.

"I bet you do. Jason is real cute." Meg smiled.

"I don't know, Meg. He's just a friend. He likes to do the things I do. Ride bikes, climb trees, and eat ice cream," Callie answered.

Callie and Meghan went into the kitchen. Mrs. Johnson was waiting with two aprons for Callie and Meghan. Callie's apron had a picture of a cat that looked just like Mr. Kitty—and Miss Kitty, too. The cat was wearing a chef's hat. Meghan's apron was lavender—just like her room—with white lace around the edge.

"I have all the ingredients measured for you

girls," Mrs. Johnson said. "All you have to do is mix them together."

Mr. Kitty wanted to be in on the baking, too. He rubbed against Meghan's legs and meowed loudly.

"Mr. Kitty," Meghan said, "brownies are for people, not cats!"

"Be careful not to spill any flour on him," Callie warned. "Or he'll look more like Jason's cat, Jack, than Miss Kitty!"

The girls licked the bowl while Mrs. Johnson put the pan in the oven.

"They'll be done in about half an hour," Mrs. Johnson said. "That'll leave just enough time for them to cool before your mom gets here, Callie."

After they cleaned up the brownie-making mess, the girls went for a bike ride and then sat in the rockers on the front porch to talk. It seemed strange to Callie that she had been gone from Greenville for only a short while. But now she and Meg didn't have a lot to talk about anymore.

"Meg, do you remember when we were real small and stayed with Grandmama while our

moms went to a class in Atlanta?" Callie asked.

"Oh yeah! Your grandmama let us play with mud pies on the back porch. We had so much fun. Then she had to give us a bath before our moms got back. Your grandmama is a lot of fun. It's almost like she never got older." Meghan smiled at the memory.

Callie smiled to herself. It really was like Grandmama was still a kid. She liked to color with Callie and to play with tea sets. Callie really missed Grandmama and Papa. *I wish they would move to Cornelius with us*, Callie thought.

"Callie, honey," Mrs. Johnson said, shaking Callie out of her daydream. "Your mom's on the phone."

Callie went inside to take the phone.

"Hi, Mom. How is Grandmama?" Callie asked first thing.

"She's doing really good. Nothing else is broken," Mom said. "Dr. James said she could go home today instead of waiting till tomorrow. I'm going to get her home, then I'll run over to pick you up. We'll go by the store to get something special for supper. How's that?"

"That sounds great. I'll be waiting for you,"

Callie said. "Oh, we made Grandmama some brownies. Don't tell her. I want it to be a surprise. OK?"

"I won't tell. See you in just a little while. I love you!" Mom said before hanging up.

"Love you, too, Mom. I'll be waiting for you," Callie said.

Callie hung up the phone and went back to the porch, where Mrs. Johnson and Meghan were.

"Grandmama is getting out of the hospital now. Mom is going to take her home and then come get me. Isn't that great?" Callie asked.

"Sure is. I know your mother is very happy with all this. Now you two can spend the night with your grandmama," Mrs. Johnson said. "I think I'll go in and put the brownies on a plate for you."

Callie looked at Meg, who was all of a sudden very quiet. *What's wrong with Meg?* Callie wondered.

Chapter Nine

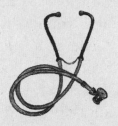

"What's wrong, Meg? You look unhappy about something."

"I just didn't want you to have to go so soon. I wanted to play awhile longer. Do you think your mom would let you stay a little longer?" Meghan looked at Callie with sad eyes.

"Well, we have a while. They haven't left the hospital yet. So what do you want to do?" Callie asked her best friend.

Callie and Meghan sat on the porch for a while. Then they walked down to the school where they both would have gone in the fall if Callie hadn't moved.

"You know, I miss not having you to talk to or play with. It really made me mad when I came to your house and saw that you had a new best friend," Meghan said in a low voice.

"MEGHAN!" Callie yelled. "Jason is a good friend. But you'll always be my best friend. I know you have other friends, too. That doesn't make me mad." Callie was a little surprised to hear Meg say that she was jealous of Jason.

"Well, I was. I'm sorry, Callie. I just didn't think you'd find another friend as soon as you moved in to your new house," Meghan said.

"I really didn't find him. He found me. He kinda grows on you." Callie laughed.

Both girls laughed as they started back up the street to Meghan's house. They passed the house Callie and her parents used to live in when they were in Greenville. Somebody else was living there now. Meg didn't know who it was. Just that they had a *boy*.

"Maybe you should get to know him, Meg! He might turn out to be another Jason," Callie suggested just as she saw her Mom pull into Meghan's driveway.

"Oh, we'd better hurry. Your mom's here." Meg grabbed Callie's hand so they could run up the hill to her house.

Callie and Meg ran up just as Callie's mom was getting out of the Jeep.

"Hello, where have you two been?" she asked, hugging both girls.

"Oh, just down to the school and by our old house," Callie answered.

"We need to get a move on, Miss Callie," Mom said. "Papa is getting hungry. I told him that you and I would go to the store. Let me go in and say hello to Meg's mom. Then we'll be on our way."

Callie and Meg stayed out by the car.

"I can't believe it's time for you to go. We didn't have time to do much," Meghan said.

"I know, Meg. I wish we lived closer so we could be together more. Maybe Mom will let me call you later. I don't think we're going back tonight." Callie smiled at her best friend.

Callie's Mom came back out with Mrs. Johnson and the brownies. "Callie, did you thank Mrs. Johnson for letting you make the brownies and for lunch?" she asked.

"Oh, I did, Mom. But thank you again, Mrs. Johnson. I really liked lunch and the paddle boat ride." Callie gave Mrs. Johnson a hug.

"Oh, sweetie, you are very welcome. Any-time you want to come down, just let me know." She gave Callie a kiss on the top of her head.

Callie and Meghan said a sad good-bye, then Callie got in the Jeep with Mom. They both waved as they went down the hill to the main road.

"Mom, do you miss living here?" Callie asked.

"Sure I do, Callie. I lived here all my life. But I also like where we live now. We've made a lot of good friends. Sometimes change is for the best. Sometimes it helps you grow."

They stopped at the store to pick up a few things for supper and to get Grandmama some flowers. Callie found a coloring book that she thought Grandmama would like and asked if they could get it.

"Sure, I think that would be really nice. You and Grandmama can sit on the sun porch and color."

Back in the Jeep, Callie told her mom about how Meghan had been mad at her because of Jason. "I don't understand why, Mom. It's not like I found Jason. He found me," Callie said in a funny voice that made Mom turn to look at her.

"Honey, sometimes change is just as hard for the people around us as it is for us. Meg was just sad that you had a new friend and that you weren't here with her as you've always been," Mom explained.

They soon arrived at Grandmama's house. Papa was sitting on the wide front porch, reading the Sunday paper. Callie loved the big old house, with its double front doors and dark gray shutters. This was what she wanted her house to look like someday.

"Callie Ann, how in the world are you?" Papa asked as he met the Jeep in the driveway. "I've been waiting for you."

Callie couldn't wait to get out of the Jeep to hug her papa.

"Love you, love you, love you!" Papa said, picking Callie up and swinging her around.

"I love you too, Papa. You've been working in the yard. Just look at all the new flowers," Callie said, hugging Papa tight.

Flowers were just one of the things Callie loved about going to Grandmama and Papa's house. She loved tulips as much as they did.

Papa had always put in a new bed every year.

"Your grandmama is waiting for you in the sun-room. She wants to show you a really special flower bed. Come on, I'll go with you," Papa told Callie. He turned to Callie's mom. "Oh, Sara, do you need any help with the bags?"

"No, Papa. You two go ahead. I'm fine." Mom smiled.

Callie wondered why Papa had winked at Mom and why Mom was smiling so big. Did they know something she didn't?

Chapter Ten

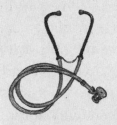

Callie and Papa found Grandmama just where Papa said she would be. The sun-room was one of Callie's favorites in the whole house. It was big, with windows on three sides. You could look out on the backyard and see all Grandmama and Papa's flowers.

"Well, honey bunch, there you are," Grandmama said as Callie and Papa walked into the room. "Come give me a hug."

Grandmama was a small woman, with hair and eyes just like Callie's. Everybody said that Callie was the spitting image of her grandmama. Callie liked that.

"How is your ankle, Grandmama?" Callie asked, giving Grandmama a big hug.

"It hurts just a bit, but I'm going to be fine," Grandmama told Callie.

"Papa said you wanted to show me something. What is it?" Callie asked, her green eyes wide.

"Yes, we have a new flower bed. You can see it from here. Do you see where the little bunny is hopping?" Grandmama asked.

"Yes, ma'am," Callie said.

"Well, your papa and I went over to your old house and asked if we could have the tulips that were in your birthday bed. The folks were real nice. We told them how you had gotten red tulips for your birthday every year since you were born. They said we could have them. So now your birthday flowers are all right here so Papa and I can watch them grow."

"Oh, Grandmama, Papa. Thank you so much. Oh, Mom, did you hear? My red tulips are all right here with Grandmama and Papa." Callie squealed with delight as her mom came into the sun-room.

"Yes, I know, Miss Callie," Mom said. "You are a lucky little girl. Grandmama and Papa love you lots. So do your daddy and I. Now let's you

and I fix supper for Grandmama and Papa. Then you can show Grandmama what you bought at the store for you two to do this evening."

Callie and her mom fixed supper for everybody. They ate brownies for dessert.

"Mom, did Dr. James say anything about Jamie before you and Grandmama left the hospital?" Callie asked while they cleaned up after supper.

"No, but I did talk to her mom. She gave me Jamie's address so you could write to her after we get back home."

"I just hope she's all right. I'll pray for her," Callie said. "Right now I'm going to show Grandmama our coloring book. Are we through in here?"

"We are, Miss Callie. You go right ahead and color with Grandmama."

Callie smiled as she went to get the coloring book and to find Grandmama. Today had been a good day. Grandmama was going to be OK. And she had made another friend.

Series for Young Readers*
From Bethany House Publishers

★ ★ ★

THE ADVENTURES OF CALLIE ANN
by Shannon Mason Leppard
Readers will giggle their way through the true-to-life escapades of Callie Ann Davies and her many North Carolina friends.

★ ★ ★

BACKPACK MYSTERIES
by Mary Carpenter Reid
This excitement-filled mystery series follows the mishaps and adventures of Steff and Paulie Larson as they strive to help often-eccentric relatives crack their toughest cases.

★ ★ ★

THE CUL-DE-SAC KIDS
by Beverly Lewis
Each story in this lighthearted series features the hilarious antics and predicaments of nine endearing boys and girls who live on Blossom Hill Lane.

★ ★ ★

RUBY SLIPPERS SCHOOL
by Stacy Towle Morgan
Join the fun as home-schoolers Hope and Annie Brown visit fascinating countries and meet inspiring Christians from around the world!

★ ★ ★

THREE COUSINS DETECTIVE CLUB®
by Elspeth Campbell Murphy
Famous detective cousins Timothy, Titus, and Sarah-Jane learn compelling Scripture-based truths while finding—and solving—intriguing mysteries.

* (ages 7–10)